CLOUDS
for Breakfast

BY LAURA EISEN

ILLUSTRATED BY KENT CISSNA

Published by StarryBooks, LLC
Yelm, Washington 98597
U.S.A.
www.cloudsforbreakfast.com

StarryBooks and Colophon are trademarks of StarryBooks, LLC
www.StarryBooks.net

Based on an original story by Laura Eisen
Illustrations by Kent Cissna
Design by Melissa Peizer
Edited by Pat Richker and Jaime Leal-Anaya
Spanish Translation by Valeria Zimmerman and Jose Antonio Ayala Schmitt
Photography by Mark Frey

Library of Congress Cataloging-in-Publication Data
Eisen, Laura.
Clouds for Breakfast
by Laura Eisen.
Illustrated by Kent Cissna

ISBN   978-0-988-21137-7
eISBN 978-0-988-21130-8

Summary: Children create a day of imaginative adventures inspired by
the ever-changing nature of clouds.

ISBN 978-0-988-21137-7   (trade)
[1.Clouds-Fiction] 1. Title
[2.Imagination

Printed in the United States of America
First Edition
February 2013

www.StarryBooks.net
www.cloudsforbreakfast.com

A percentage of the sale of each book will be donated to the Phoenix Rising School,
dedicated to inspiring students to become self-empowered individuals.

To JZ Knight and Ramtha the Enlightened One,
for their knowledge and inspiration to create our dreams.

To our children Josh, Elizabeth, Diego Antonio, and Stella Eden,
and to all children for dreaming the future.

Clouds for breakfast,
that's how I start my day.
Clouds for breakfast,
and then I'm on my way.

I fill my spoon
with many puffs
of purple, pink, and gold,
and soon my adventures
begin to unfold.

I soar like a giant bird
riding an ocean breeze.

I sail over lakes
and streams
high above the trees.

One moment I'm a tiger,

stalking in the sky.

Then stretching,

I become . . .

A winged butterfly.

I race over mountaintops
all covered in snow.
The world is full of wonders
that I have yet to know.

Clouds for breakfast
are filled with surprises.
Clouds for breakfast
come in all colors
and all sizes.

I heap my spoon with
lots of clouds
giant, dark, and gray,
and I am a thunderstorm
with rain on the way.
I'm bolts of lightning,
loud thunder crashing.

I'm making

lots of puddles

for splishing and splashing.

After the storm is through,

the clouds drift to and fro,

and shining

all through them

is the brightest rainbow.

Some days
I pile my spoon
with clouds
all fluffy, soft, and white.

I'm filled with falling snow
and the children I delight.

I scatter snowflakes
everywhere,
I make things disappear.

And beneath that
frosty blanket
dreams of spring
are bright and clear.

Clouds for breakfast,
my spoon overflows
with fun.
Today I'll play a game
of hide-and-seek with
the sun.
And just when it seems
that the clouds are here
to stay . . .

I'll open
the cloud curtains
to let the sun come out
and play.

Clouds for breakfast
are different every morn.
Clouds for breakfast
can be any shape or form.

Some mornings
I'm a checkerboard
filling up the skies.

And when a great
wind blows
I'm a dozen dragonflies.

In every cloud
there is a face
that I can clearly see,
a cat, a dog,
a ram, a frog . . .

And sometimes . . .
even me!

Clouds for breakfast,
each day begins anew.
I know there isn't anything
that I can't be or do.

I love clouds for breakfast,
they remind me of me,
always changing,
always different,
always wild and free.

Now I'm full from
clouds for breakfast,
my day has been
quite fine.
I've imagined
and adventured
through the magic
of my mind.

I'm full from
clouds for breakfast,
so tonight I'll fill my spoon
with lots of
shimmering stars
and a shiny slice of moon.